Gigi loves Ella...

that's no lie...

More than a birdie
way up in the sky!

More than the sunshine
in the sky above...

or a couple little duckies
that are falling in love!

More than a kitty cat

singing a song...

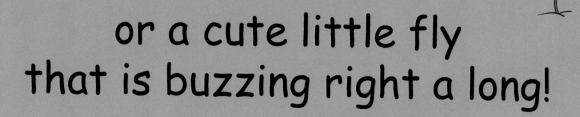

or a cute little fly
that is buzzing right a long!

More than a donkey,

happy as can be...

or a little baby cow,

that is looking at a bee!

More than a horsey

wearing a suit...

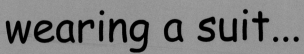

or a cow that has a dress on

That would really be a hoot!

Pops loves Ella,

that's no lie...

More than some horses

running in a race...

or a bunny with a snorkle

and a mask on his face!

More than a hippo,

with an ice cream cone ...

or a doggy that is chewing

on a great, big bone!

More than zebra

with a polka-dot coat ...

or a little pirate duckie
on a teeny, tiny boat!

When the stars shine bright ...

or the sky is blue ...

Gigi loves Ella...

Pops loves her too!

Sally was born in Jackson, Michigan. She has lived all over the country with her husband, Fred. They have 3

grown children. She has written over 30 children's books and had her first book published in 2000.

Loves You Books are all sweet and simple rhyming books with really cute illustrations.

You can see more at: lovesyoubooks.com

Made in the USA
Las Vegas, NV
24 May 2021